each

help

other

play

www.rourkepublishing.com

Edited by Luana K. Mitten
Illustrated by Anita DuFalla
Art Direction and Page Layout by Renee Brady

Photo Credits: ©

Library of Congress Cataloging-in-Publication Data

Greve, Meg
 Kick, Pass, SCORE! / Meg Greve.
    p. cm. -- (Little Birdie Books)
 Includes bibliographical references and index.
 ISBN 978-1-61741-804-4 (hard cover) (alk. paper)
 ISBN 978-1-61236-008-9 (soft cover)
 Library of Congress Control Number: 2011924656

Rourke Publishing
Printed in China, Voion Industry
   Guangdong Province
042011
042011LP

www.rourkepublishing.com - rourke@rourkepublishing.com
Post Office Box 643328 Vero Beach, Florida 32964

Kick, Pass, SCORE!

By Meg Greve
Illustrated by Anita DuFalla

The Lions and Monkeys play soccer after school.

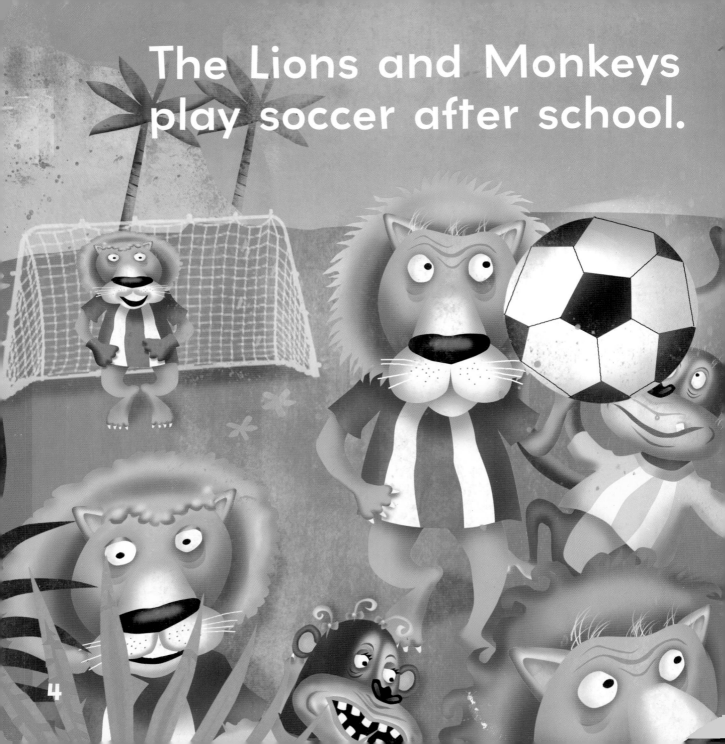

The Monkeys never win.

"Me, me! Pass to me!" yells Marty Monkey.

6

Molly Monkey
runs by him
and trips
on the ball.

The Lions win.

9

The school bell rings. It's time to play soccer.

11

"Me, me! Pass to me!" yells Molly Monkey.

Marty Monkey runs by her and falls down.

13

The Lions win again.

Molly and Marty are mad. "You don't pass the ball," says Molly.

"You don't pass the ball," says Marty.

"Let's help each other," says Molly.

"Let's pass to each other," says Marty.

Marty and Molly kick, pass, and SCORE.

20

Monkeys WIN!

After Reading Activities

You and the Story...

Why did the monkeys keep losing?

What did Molly and Marty do to solve the problem?

Have you ever played on a team before?

What would you do to be a good team player?

Words You Know Now...

Tell your friend a sentence using the words you know now.

ball
each
help
other
play

You Could... Plan to Play Your Favorite Game with a Friend or Friends

- Make a list of the rules of the game.

- What will you need to play the game?

- Where will you play the game?

About the Author

Meg Greve lives in Chicago with her husband, daughter, and son. She loves to watch her children play team sports, whether they win or lose!

About the Illustrator

Acclaimed for its versatility in style, Anita DuFalla's work has appeared in many educational books, newspaper articles, and business advertisements and on numerous posters, book and magazine covers, and even giftwraps. Anita's passion for pattern is evident in both her artwork and her collection of 400 patterned tights. She lives in the Friendship neighborhood of Pittsburgh, Pennsylvania with her son, Lucas.

10